# Princess Sparkle-Heart gets a MAKEOVER

Josh Schneider

CLARION BOOKS ● Houghton Mifflin Harcourt ● Boston   New York

Clarion Books
215 Park Avenue South
New York, New York 10003

Clarion Books is an imprint of Houghton Mifflin Harcourt Publishing Company.

www.hmhbooks.com

The illustrations in this book were done in watercolor and pen and ink.
The text was set in ITC Souvenir Std.
Book design by Opal Roengchai

Library of Congress Cataloging-in-Publication Data
Schneider, Josh, 1980–
Princess Sparkle-Heart gets a makeover / Josh Schneider.
pages cm
Summary: Amelia and her best friend, Princess Sparkle-Heart,
do almost everything together, so when the Princess suffers an accident,
Amelia's mother puts her sewing box to good use and makes the doll better than ever.
ISBN 978-0-544-14228-2 (hardcover)
[1. Dolls—Repairing—Fiction.] I. Title.
PZ7.S36335Pri 2014
[E]—dc23
2013004355

Manufactured in China
SCP 10 9 8 7 6 5 4 3 2 1
4500449183

To Dana

GRRRRRRRRRRRRRRRRRRRRRF

Amelia and Princess Sparkle-Heart were best friends.

RRRRRRRRRRRRRRRRRRRRRRRRRRRRRRRRRRRRRRRRRRRRR

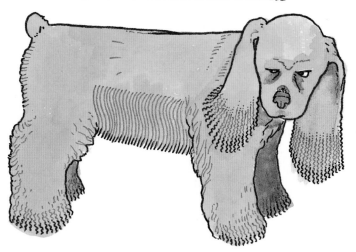

They had tea parties together.

GRRRRRRRRRRRRRRRRRRRRRRRRRRRRRRRRRRF

They went to royal weddings together.

ATLAS

GRRRRRRRRRR

RED

THIS END UP

AMELIA

RRRRRRRRRRRRRRRRRRRRRRR RRRRRRRRRR

10

They kept secrets together.

RRRRRRRRRRRRRRRRRRRRRRRRRRRRRRRRRRRRRRRRRRRRRRRRRRRRRRRRRRRRRRR

They did *almost* everything together.

GRRRRF

But one day Princess Sparkle-Heart had an accident.

Amelia was so sad. She cried and cried.
"Don't worry," said Amelia's mother.
"We'll soon have her back together, good
as new. Go get my sewing box."

"First we need to put her stuffing back in,"
said Amelia's mother.

"Put in some extra," said Amelia. "She needs
more muscles. For protection."

"Now we'll put her face back together,"
said Amelia's mother. "Look through my
sewing box and find some good buttons
for eyes."

Amelia looked through the sewing box.
She had a hard time picking just two.

"Now her mouth," said Amelia.

"Give her some good teeth."

"What about her hair?" asked her mother.

"Red hair, like mine," said Amelia.

All that was left was to find Princess Sparkle-Heart
some new clothes. Amelia gathered up all the magazines
in the house and looked for just the right outfit.

"There," said Amelia's mother.

"She's as good as new."

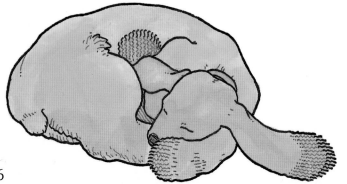

But she was wrong. Princess Sparkle-Heart
was not as good as new.

She was better.

The end